PICTURE BOOKS

Belinda
and the

GLASS
Slipper

by AMY YOUNG

viking

For Emily and Molly

VIKING

Published by Penguin Group

Penguin Young Readers Group, 345 Hudson Street, New York, New York 10014, U.S.A.

Penguin Books Ltd, Registered Offices: 80 Strand, London WC2R 0RL, England

First published in 2006 by Viking, a division of Penguin Young Readers Group

1 3 5 7 9 10 8 6 4 2

Copyright © Amy Young, 2006

LIBRARY OF CONGRESS CATALOGING-IN-PUBLICATION DATA

Young, Amy.

Belinda and the glass slipper / by Amy Young; illustrations by Amy Young.

p. cm.

Summary: Belinda competes with a very ambitious new dancer for the title role in the ballet "Cinderella."

ISBN 0-670-06082-8 (hardcover)

[1. Ballet dancers—Fiction. 2. Foot—Fiction. 3. Size—Fiction. 4. Dancing—Fiction.] I. Title.

PZ7.Y845Bdu 2006

[E]—dc22

2005022812

Manufactured in China

Set in Mrs. Eaves Roman and Weehah

Belinda was nervous.
She was about to audition
for the Grand Metropolitan
Ballet's production of
"Cinderella."

The maestro beamed. "Ah, Belinda. I am so glad you are here! Meet our newest dancer, Miss Lola Mudge. I will choose one of you for the role of Cinderella."

Lola smiled sweetly at Belinda and said, "I really want this part, and I *always* get what I want. Plus, I have perfect, tiny feet—just right for Cinderella."

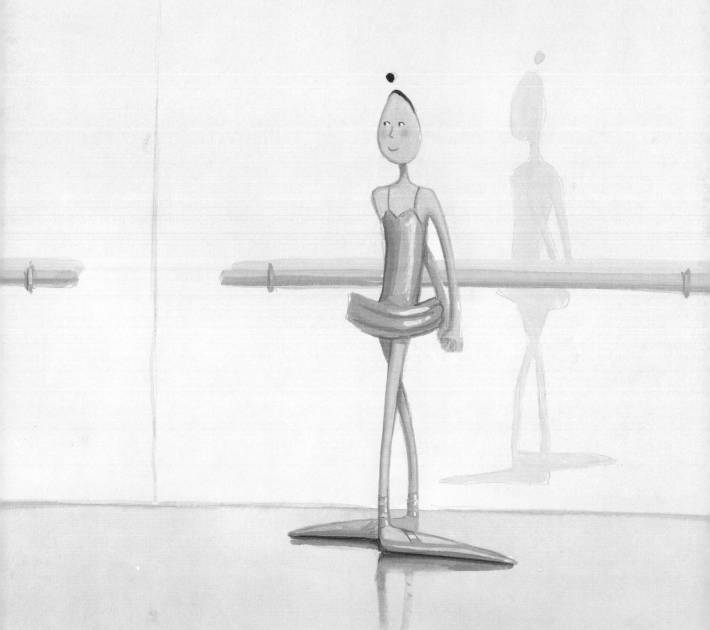

Belinda had perfect feet, too, but they happened to be huge.

"Here we go!" announced the maestro. The music started.

Lola leapt high,   but not as high as Belinda.

Lola spun fast,

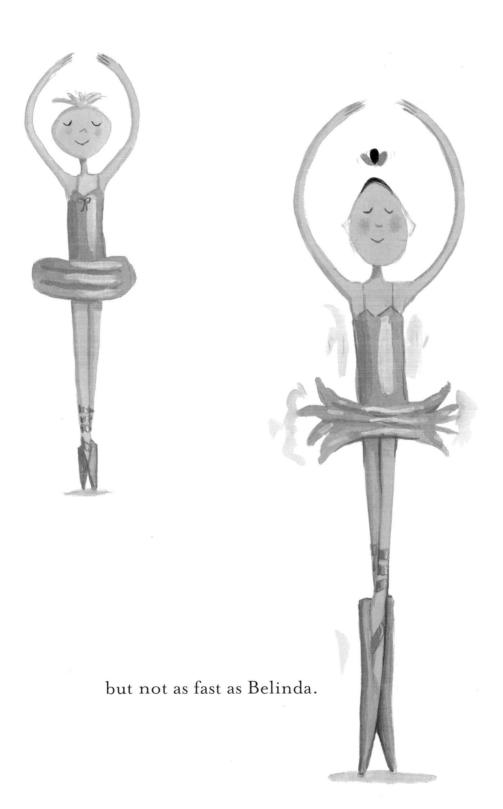

but not as fast as Belinda.

Lola was graceful, but not as graceful as Belinda,

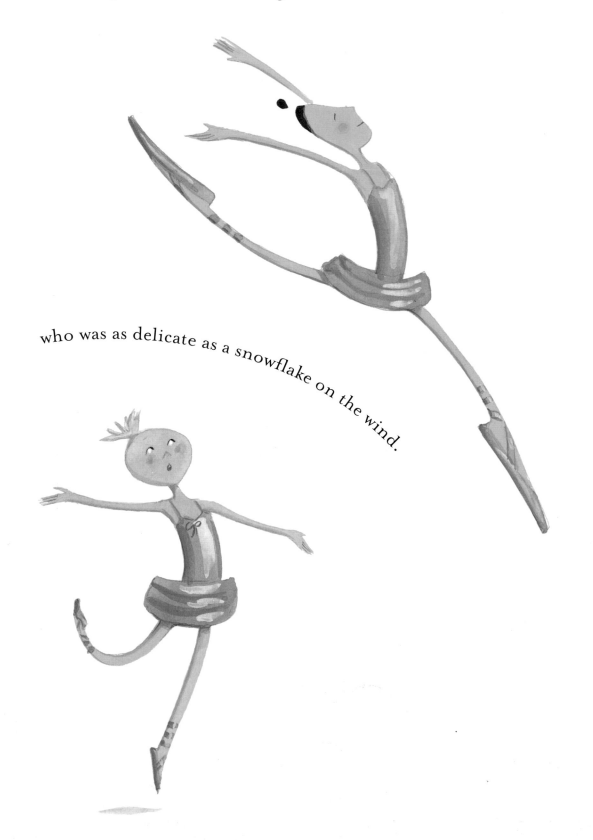

who was as delicate as a snowflake on the wind.

"Thank you, girls!" said the maestro. "You were both
excellent. Belinda, congratulations—you will be Cinderella.
Miss Mudge, you will be one of the ladies at the ball."

"That's not fair!"
Lola muttered.

They rehearsed for weeks. The other dancers didn't like practicing with Lola. When the maestro wasn't looking, she pushed them out of their *pliés* and reviled their *relevés*.

Finally it was opening night. All of the dancers bustled about, putting on costumes, tying toe shoes, and limbering up.

Lola said to Belinda, "Can you help me reach my, um, hair ribbon? It's in here, high on a shelf." Belinda followed Lola into a little closet. When she turned around to help Lola, she heard the door slam and click shut.

Lola had locked her in!

"Let me out!" cried Belinda. She had to dance! But everyone was hurrying to get onstage, and no one heard her.

Lola stole Belinda's glass slippers. They were not really made of glass, but they were bright and shiny. Lola ran off to find the maestro. "Belinda is sick, and she asked me to dance her part," she lied.

"Oh dear, the poor child! But how can you take her place?
You will have to wear the glass slippers in the ball scene,
and they'll be much too big for you," said the maestro.

"I'll make them fit," said Lola.

She crammed lots of stuffing into the glass slippers and stashed them with a fancy costume for the ball. She put a rag over her tutu to make herself look like Cinderella.

Then she hurried onstage just as the curtain opened.

Lola began to dance. She knew the steps, but the maestro
wished she could *jeté* a little higher, the way Belinda did.
He wished she *glissaded* more gracefully, like Belinda.

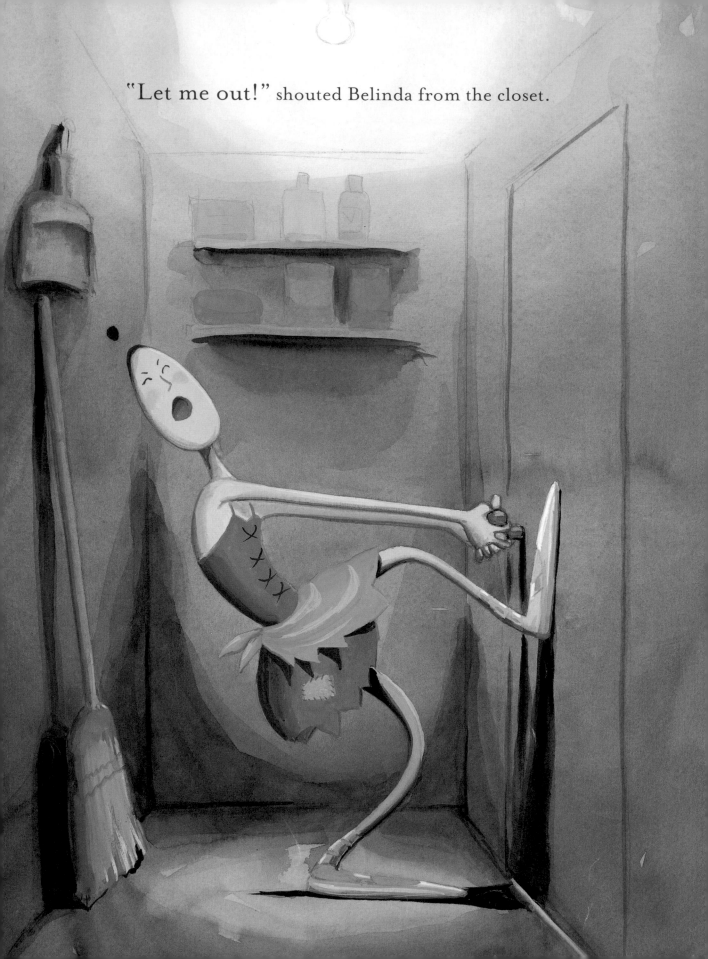

"Let me out!" shouted Belinda from the closet.

Just then, the Fairy Godmother dancer came by and heard Belinda. She unlocked the door and said, "What are you doing in there? The ball is about to begin." She helped Belinda into her tutu.

"Thank you!" Belinda said. "But where are my glass slippers?"

"I don't know," said the Fairy Godmother dancer. "Just wear what you've got on. Hurry—there's no time to lose!"

Belinda stepped onto the stage just as the ball was getting
started. Every ballerina got to dance with the prince. When
it was Belinda's turn, he swept her into his arms and they
did a gorgeous *pas de deux*. The audience oohed and ahhed.

"*I'm* Cinderella," said Lola as she swooped in to claim her dance with the prince, wearing Belinda's glass slippers.

The prince frowned.

As Lola leapt and spun, something odd happened to the glass slippers. They wavered and wobbled and began to unravel! Pieces of stuffing fell out, and her feet seemed to shrink. The clock struck twelve.

Lola ran off the stage on her teeny tiny
feet, leaving behind a big glass slipper.

Soon it was time for all of the ballerinas to try on the glass slipper. When the prince found the foot that fit the slipper, he would know that he had found his true love—Cinderella. One by one the dancers tried it on, but no one's foot fit.

Just before it was Belinda's turn, Lola pushed her out of the way. She stuck her foot in the slipper, but of course it was much too big for her, now that the stuffing was gone. "Just pretend it fits!" Lola hissed at the prince.

Belinda had had enough. She stepped up and curtsied gracefully before the prince. He smiled happily at her and knelt to try the slipper on her foot.

It fit perfectly.

Lola was furious. She stomped up to Belinda and said, "The prince is mine! I want him! And I *always* get what I want!"

"Not this time," said Belinda.

Lola tried to crush Belinda's foot
with her heel, but Belinda
pirouetted out of reach.

Lola sprang after her, but Belinda
protected herself with a well-executed
battement,

and she escaped with
a stunningly brilliant
tour en l'air.

Belinda dazzled the audience, soaring over their heads like a rainbow. Lola sank into a heap. She knew she had lost.

Belinda floated into the prince's arms.

The ballet was a great success. Everyone said it was one of the best they'd seen. So different! So full of action and emotion!

The maestro took all the dancers out for cake and hot chocolate. Everyone had a good time except for Lola, who decided she didn't want to be a dancer after all.

She left the ballet to become a hockey player.

She was nicknamed "Teensy Toes" because her feet were so small. She got into a lot of fights, but she also won a lot of games.